A HOUSE DIVIDED

Written by Neil Morris
Illustrated by Simon Howden

Scholastic Publications Ltd.,
10 Earlham Street, London WC2H 9RX, UK
First published in the UK by Scholastic Publications Limited, 1988
Copyright © 1987 King Features Entertainment, Inc./King Features Syndicate, Inc.
Distribution by Yaffa Character Licensing, London
DEFENDERS OF THE EARTH and associated characters are trademarks owned
by and used under licence from King Features Syndicate Inc.

ISBN 0 590 70909 7

Made and printed in Hong Kong
Typeset in Times Roman by AKM Associates (UK) Ltd,
Ajmal House, Hayes Road, Southall, London

Hippo Books
Scholastic Publications Ltd
London

Ming the Merciless stood at the great windows of his throne room. He was deep in thought, and did not even hear Octon approach.

"Sire, are you sure you wouldn't prefer to use a robot?" asked the eight-legged machine.

"I am sure, Octon," Ming replied sharply. "I have thought this through very carefully. The earthling has a powerful motive for doing as I wish."

Octon was still not totally convinced. "But Sire," he pleaded, "it's such a vast power, and humans are so . . . undependable."

"Silence, Octon!" roared Ming, as he walked over to the throne. "The human will not fail me. Send him in now."

At this command, a door quietly slid open at the far end of the throne room. Two ice robots dragged in a bearded man and placed him before Ming. The man lifted his head and stared at his powerful captor.

"Who . . . who are you?" he stammered.

"I am Ming the Merciless," came the strong reply. "And it humours me to grant you a wish."

At these words the man's face hardened with hatred. "I have only one wish," he said. "And that is to destroy the Phantom!"

Ming was pleased with the man's reply. He stood up at his throne and pointed to a golden chamber gliding through the room towards them. "Enter the chamber, earthling, and your wish will be granted!" he cried.

The chamber stopped before the man, and at once its doors opened. The man hesitated for a moment, and then quickly entered the chamber. The doors closed, and immediately the man was surrounded by flashes of vivid colour as energy waves bored into him. Yellow smoke clouded the chamber, when suddenly the doors burst open. The bearded man had been transformed into a demon-like creature!

"You are now N'Dama, the demon god of weather," Ming shouted in a devilish voice. "For the next twenty-four hours you will have all the

power you need to defeat your brother, the
Phantom. Go now, and destroy him!"

. . . . . .

In their communications room, Rick Gordon
and L.J. sat at the control panel watching a
news report.

"In the last five days," reported the
newswoman, "the tropics of Africa have been
plagued with rain, wind and snow. Scientists are
puzzled and the inhabitants, the Bandar
bushmen, are in a state of despair."

Mandrake the Magician also heard the news
report. "Phantom! Jedda!" he called. "There is
news about your home in Africa."

As the Phantom watched the report, he saw huge black clouds gather into the shape of a skull. Without a word, the Phantom and Jedda were gone.

"Where did *they* go?" asked L.J. "I didn't even see them leave!"

"Those black clouds couldn't be natural," said Rick Gordon. "They seemed more like some kind of threat."

"A threat from one who can control the clouds cannot be easily ignored!" said Mandrake gravely.

"Then we must help the Phantom and Jedda!" cried Rick.

"No, Rick," said Mandrake. "Their family home is being threatened, and that makes it a personal challenge. Unless they ask for our help, the Phantom and Jedda will face this threat alone."

· · · · · ·

In the African tropics, the Bandar people suffered as never before. Above them the sky was black with rainclouds and thunder. Suddenly they saw a strange figure appear on a mountain top.

"Hear ye and tremble!" roared a voice like thunder itself. "I, N'Dama, spirit demon of the winds, have come back to my ancestral home to rule this land and its people as I choose. Obey me without question!"

Guran, chief of the Bandar people, felt he recognized something about the demon. "We follow only the teachings of our elders," he yelled up at N'Dama. "You are not a spirit, but a bad child. Leave us, or the eyes of the

9

Phantom will know your deeds!"

At these challenging words, N'Dama swooped down from the mountain to stand before the people. He looked Chief Guran straight in the face and spoke with venom. "I challenge your Phantom! But no one has seen him for many moons. He has left you!"

Guran remained calm. "The Phantom is our friend and brother," he replied firmly. "He will never fail us."

N'Dama threw his hands in the air, and at once the sky turned black. "Fool!" he cried. "By nightfall you and your people will be my subjects, or else you will be destroyed. The choice is yours!"

Then, like a bolt of lightning, N'Dama was gone. Guran tried not to appear worried as he murmured to himself, "Phantom, my friend, if ever your people needed you, it is now. . . ."

. . . . . .

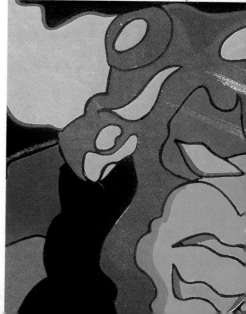

Guran could not know it, but the Phantom and Jedda were heading for Africa at that very moment. "It's important that the Bandar know I will always stand by them," the Phantom told Jedda, as he steered their jet helicopter.

"And as a future Phantom," said Jedda, "I'll also do whatever I can, father."

As the jet-copter started to come in to land, storm clouds gathered together and surrounded the craft. Suddenly there were black clouds everywhere, forming the evil features of N'Dama. The 'copter started to shake wildly in

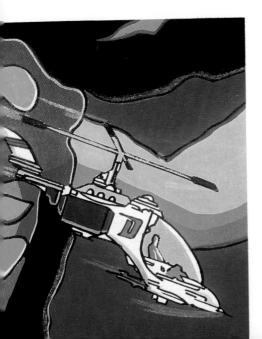

the turbulent air, and the Phantom fought for control. But as he did so, the electrical system failed and the engine started to sputter. The Phantom knew he would have to make an emergency landing, but just then lightning blasted the tail rudder and the helicopter went into an uncontrollable spin.

There was nothing the Phantom could do. He quickly shouted to Jedda to jump, and they both ejected from the cockpit. They fell at great speed towards the jungle below, but in the nick of

time, just before hitting the ground, both grabbed the same tree branch. After a few somersaults, father and daughter landed gently in a catlike crouch. As they stood up, they heard their helicopter crash nearby, and ducked for safety as parts of the broken craft came hurtling towards them.

Then they heard N'Dama's evil voice. "Well done, Phantom," he jeered. "But the real test of your worth is yet to come! It's been twenty years since we last met, but this time things will be different!"

In their council chamber, the Bandar leaders were trying to decide on a course of action. Some wanted to move their people to caves in the hills, others urged that they do as the weather demon commanded. But Guran, their chief, knew no fear. "For four hundred years the Phantom has stood by us," he said. "He will not fail us in our hour of need."

Some councillors were still not in agreement, but as they spoke, a young boy ran through the village towards the council chamber, shouting frantically. "He's here! The Phantom is coming!" the boy yelled.

And it was true. As the Phantom and Jedda galloped into the village on Hero, the Phantom's white stallion, Guran rushed out to greet them.

"Phantom! Jedda!" he cried. "I only wish your homecoming were in happier circumstances."

Guran at once told the Phantom of the demon god, N'Dama. "He knows you well," said Guran, "and waits for you in Skull Cave."

"I know no N'Dama," replied the Phantom. "But no one will desecrate my home!" He and Jedda mounted Hero and sped off at once.

Bolts of lightning struck the ground around them as they rode, but Hero kept them right on course until they reached Skull Cave.

As they entered the cave, the Phantom saw a strange figure sitting on the throne. "Can it be?" he asked, shocked. "Is it really you?"

"Yes," came the mocking reply. "It's your dear older brother, Kurt. And this time I'll get the title that's due to me!"

The Phantom had hoped never to see his brother again, and Jedda did not even know of his existence. "I don't understand," she said, looking at her father.

"I wanted you to know nothing of this," the Phantom told Jedda gently. "But now I will explain."

"Oh do, brother dear," scoffed Kurt. "You do so like telling stories."

"It all started the day our father put us to the ultimate test," the Phantom began. "We were just boys then. Father asked the two of us to go to the shrine on Mount M'Tanga and bring the Jewel of Zandoon down for a Bandar ceremony. He said this test would determine which of us would become the next Phantom after him.

"My brother Kurt asked to go alone. 'Kit will only get in the way,' he said. But father insisted that we learn to work with others. As soon as we set off, Kurt said we should have a race to see who could get the Jewel first. It angered me that my brother wanted to race, but I knew I could win, so I agreed.

"As we ran through the jungle towards Mount M'Tanga, we met our first danger — a ferocious lion. Kurt threw a rock at the beast and it charged straight at him. I hid in the tall grass as Kurt just managed to scamper up a tree to escape the lion. I could see that he was safe there, and thought of leaving him so that I could win the race. But then I remembered that Father wanted us to work as a team, so I yelled at the lion from the undergrowth. He soon came after me, but as I ran off I heard Kurt laughing. 'See you, little brother,' he shouted, 'when I get home with the Jewel of Zandoon!'

"I leapt into the river to get away from the lion, and then struggled on towards the

mountain. When at last I got to the foot of the
mountain, I knew that Kurt must be at least half
way up. But I was determined not to give in. I
climbed and climbed until at last I saw him
above me.

"'Give it up, Kit,' he shouted down. 'You're just
not a winner!'

" 'At least I don't have to cheat to win,'
I shouted back, and that made my brother very
angry. He stamped his foot in his rage, sending

rocks cascading down towards me. One of them
hit me, and I must have fallen unconscious,
because that's the last thing I remember till I
was back at home with my father.

"It was not long before Kurt returned with the
Jewel of Zandoon. He rushed to show it to
Father and told of the dangers he had
encountered on the way. He said that he had
fought off a fierce lion and helped me as much
as he could to climb Mount M'Tanga.

" 'But where is your brother now?' asked
Father.

" 'Father, something terrible happened,' Kurt

replied. 'Kit fell as he was climbing the mountain. I tried to save him, but I could not. I did everything I could.' Then Father told him that I was still alive.

" 'I asked Guran to follow you on your quest,' Father said. 'When you left Kit on the mountain alone, Guran carried your brother home. So I have decided to make Kit the next Phantom after I'm gone. I'm sorry, Kurt, but you have never learned that the Phantom is meant to serve others.'

" 'But I won the race!' cried Kurt. 'Besides, the oldest son always becomes the next Phantom, and I'm the oldest!'

"But Father's mind was made up, and nothing

would change it, least of all Kurt's pleading and cursing.

" 'You just wait!' Kurt screamed. 'I'll make you pay for this, little brother!'

"It was then that Kurt disappeared, vowing to get even with me one day. I tried to make him stay, but Father said that he must find his own destiny. And I have not seen my brother since.

"*That* is how it happened, Jedda. And that is why I have never spoken of my brother."

"But I am here now, dear little brother!" laughed Kurt. As he pointed a finger at the Phantom and Jedda, a terrific wind blew them across the cave.

"I hoped the years would have given you wisdom," the Phantom said to his brother. "But I see that they haven't. I feel sorry for you." Taking Jedda by the hand, the Phantom disappeared into the shadows of the cave.

Left alone, Kurt felt the eyes of his ancestors fall on their wayward son. "Stop staring at me!" he shouted at a portrait of his father. "I could have been a better Phantom than any of you. And I still will be!"

Kurt felt so threatened by the pictures that he failed to see the Phantom as he swung down on him from the roof of the cave. The Phantom booted his brother so hard that he flew towards Jedda, who was also waiting for him. She used a judo flip to slam him hard against the stone wall of the cave. But Kurt was still N'Dama, the weather demon. He picked himself up and

turned towards them. Suddenly he fired huge
balls of ice and hailstones at the Phantom and
Jedda, hitting them and knocking them to the
ground.

"Mark these moments well, dear brother,"
sneered Kurt, "for they are your last! I will
destroy you and take the title that is rightfully
mine. This is indeed my moment of triumph."

As Kurt spoke these evil words, the spirit of his father was moved. His image rose from the family portrait. "Triumph?" the spirit said in a mysterious, ghostlike voice. "Triumph? No, my son, this is your moment of shame."

Kurt struck out at the ghostly image in his rage, but the image faded into nothingness. In frustration Kurt picked up the portrait of his father and smashed it to the ground. "I am the better one!" he cried. "I should have been the Phantom, and I *will* be!"

"Never!" shouted a voice behind him. It was the Phantom, who dragged himself across the cave to lunge at his brother. As he tried to grab him, the Phantom ripped N'Dama's mask off.

"No!" screamed Kurt. "No one may see my face! No one!" His eyes were raging tornadoes, spinning madly. "If I cannot *be* the Phantom," he roared, "then I will destroy everything the Phantom stands for."

Kurt pushed the Phantom to the ground and rushed off through the cave. But when he reached the throne room, he was surprised by a group of Bandar warriors. They had finally decided to come and take up the fight against N'Dama, the weather demon.

"Attack!" cried Guran, and his warriors let loose a barrage of arrows and spears. Kurt held out his glowing hands, and a huge gust of wind blew the weapons back at his attackers. Then he fired a lightning bolt at a great slab of stone above the warriors' heads. The slab crumbled, and boulders buried the warriors alive.

At that moment the Phantom and Jedda reached the throne room. "I won't stand by and see the Bandar hurt," the Phantom told his brother.

"What can you do?" replied Kurt. "With one wave of my hand I could destroy your friend Guran."

The Phantom knew that he was right. "What do you want of me?" he asked his brother with resignation.

"I have an idea," Kurt replied calmly. "One that will appeal to your sporting nature. A race! A race for the Jewel of Zandoon!"

"Like when we were boys?" asked the Phantom in horror.

"Yes, only this time the winner becomes the Phantom — as I should have then."

Jedda appealed to her father. "Dad, you mustn't do it!" she cried.

"I have no choice," the Phantom said. "There are too many innocent lives at stake."

"Then let the race begin!" shouted Kurt in triumph.

. . . . . .

The two brothers raced out of the cave together.
But it was soon clear that it was to be no
ordinary race. Kurt held out a glowing hand,
and at once a patch of ice formed before his
brother. The Phantom slipped and fell.

"Don't leave me waiting at the altar, Kit,"
Kurt jeered.

"Not this time, Kurt. Not this time!" the
Phantom shouted, picking himself up.

They raced on, side by side, until they came to

a yawning chasm. As the Phantom reached out for a vine to swing across the abyss, Kurt created a gust of wind. The vine blew out of reach, and the Phantom slipped over the edge. He just managed to cling on by his fingertips, and looked up into his brother's riveting eyes. "Kurt? Is this how you want it to end?" he asked.

"Why, Kit," his brother joked, "I'd say you have the situation well in hand." And with that he grasped the vine to swing across.

At that same moment the Phantom dived into the chasm and grabbed his brother's legs. They both swung to the other side of the chasm.

"Thanks for the ride, pal," laughed the Phantom, slapping his brother on the back. They ran on, and now the Phantom took the lead. Seeing a herd of elephants ahead, Kurt threw up his hand and caused a flash of lightning to alarm them. Suddenly the Phantom was surrounded by stampeding elephants and a giant cloud of dust. By the time the last beast had passed, the Phantom knew that he was now well behind in the race.

"It's time I used the special powers of the Phantom," he thought, and raised his fists above his head. "By jungle law, the ghost who walks calls forth the power of ten tigers!" he cried. This call filled the Phantom with supernatural power. Surrounded by a force field, he charged off to catch his brother.

Not far behind was Jedda, who had ridden from Skull Cave on Hero, but the Phantom did not know this. She had the feeling that the race would not be a fair one, and so had followed her father.

The power of ten tigers soon helped the Phantom to catch up with his brother, who was now nearing his goal. "I must win this race," the Phantom called out. "The future of the Phantom rests with me!"

The two brothers were again running side by side. They were not far from the rim of the volcano, near the altar which housed the Jewel of Zandoon.

"Give up, Kit," cried Kurt. "It's pointless for you. I will always hold the final card."

"You hold nothing, now or ever!" shouted the Phantom, overtaking his brother and racing on. But suddenly a bolt of lightning flew over his head, stopping him in his tracks. Thunder boomed as the Phantom turned to face his attacker.

By this time Jedda had caught up with them, and she knew that she must now act quickly. "Hero!" she shouted at her horse. "Hero, hear me! I need your help!" At once a glow of power formed around the horse and his rider. Hero bolted off towards Kurt.

As he reached his enemy, Hero reared up on his hind legs. Kurt instinctively took a step backwards. He was now at the very edge of the volcano.

"Kurt! Watch out!" the Phantom cried, rushing to try and save his brother. But it was too late. Kurt went over the edge and fell headlong into the darkness of the volcano.

The Phantom was horrified. "Kurt, no!" he shouted.

"Father, I'm sorry!" said Jedda.

"It didn't have to end like this," cried the Phantom in anger and despair.

But as Kurt hurtled down to certain destruction, he called up one last ounce of strength. "Wind!" he roared. "Cushion my fall, and carry me!" At once a great blast of wind blew him on to a ledge at the side of the volcano.

Kurt was safe, but still not sorry. "You have won this time, little brother," he groaned. "But you will have to look over your shoulder every day of your life!"

. . . . . .

As Kurt cursed his fate, Ming the Merciless watched him on his monitor. He had been following the human's progress the whole time!

"I may have lost this battle," he said, stroking his beard thoughtfully, "but *he* will be back!"

THE DEFENDERS

THE PHANTOM
With strange supernatural powers taught by the natives of the Deep Woods, he draws on the strength of jungle animals and is the ultimate enemy of evil.

FLASH GORDON
The swashbuckling, square-jawed space pilot. He's fearless, resourceful, clever and strong – an intergalactic hero.

MANDRAKE THE MAGICIAN
Suave and sophisticated, moving only in the best of circles, he is adept at hypnotic deception. The master of illusion.

LOTHAR
The big, muscular but soft-spoken Jamaican is Mandrake's lifetime friend and protector. Easy-going and charming, but with fists of steel!